W9-BOM-869

ATTACK OF THE SOGGY UNDERWATER PEOPLE

Don't miss these other nail-biting **MAXimum Boy** adventures:

MAXimum Boy

starring in
ATTACK OF THE SOGGY UNDERWATER PEOPLE

BY DAN GREENBURG
ILLUSTRATIONS BY GREG SWEARINGEN

A Little Apple Paperback

SCHOLASTIC INC.
New York   Toronto   London   Auckland   Sydney
Mexico City   New Delhi   Hong Kong   Buenos Aires

If you purchased this book without a cover, you should be aware that this book is stolen property. It was reported as "unsold and destroyed" to the publisher, and neither the author nor the publisher has received any payment for this "stripped book."

No part of this publication may be reproduced in whole or in part, or stored in a retrieval system, or transmitted in any form or by any means, electronic, mechanical, photocopying, recording, or otherwise, without written permission of the publisher. For information regarding permission, write to Scholastic Inc., Attention: Permissions Department, 557 Broadway, New York, NY 10012.

ISBN 0-439-21949-3

Text copyright © 2002 by Dan Greenburg
Illustrations copyright © 2002 by Scholastic Inc.

All rights reserved. Published by Scholastic Inc.

SCHOLASTIC, LITTLE APPLE PAPERBACKS, and associated logos are trademarks and/or registered trademarks of Scholastic Inc.

12 11 10 9 8 7 6 5 4 3 2   3 4 5 6 7/0
                                         40

Printed in the U.S.A.
First Scholastic printing, May 2002

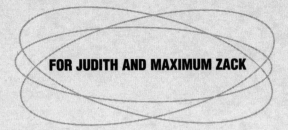

FOR JUDITH AND MAXIMUM ZACK

CHAPTER 1

Let me ask you something. Do you think it's fair to expect an eleven-year-old boy to save his whole planet? Well, neither do I, but that's just what they asked me to do.

My name is Max Silver. I'm eleven years old. I live in Chicago with my parents and my annoying sister, Tiffany. Three years ago, I accidentally handled some rocks at the Air and Space Museum that had just come from outer space. Right after that I found out I could do things that most eleven-year-olds can't. Like fly. And lift trucks over my head with one hand. And run faster than the speed of sound. And rub my belly and pat my head at the same time.

If I don't use my superpowers, I'm the second-worst athlete in the sixth grade. But if I used them, I'd blow my cover and put my family in danger. You'd think I could use just a *little* of my superpowers and be just a *little* stronger and faster than other kids, but that's not how superpowers work. With superpowers, it's all or nothing. I really hate that.

I do have a few weaknesses. I'm allergic to sweet potatoes, milk products, ragweed, and math. Even *hearing* a math problem makes me weak, dizzy, and nauseous.

Superman had the same problem with kryptonite. I'm the only kid in the sixth grade who has a doctor's excuse to get out of math.

Because of my superpowers, the President of the United States is always sending me out on missions to help our country. Like the time an evil scientist named Dr. Zirkon towed the island of Manhattan out to sea. Or the time an angry chef made everything taste like broccoli. Or the time Earth was invaded by evil cattle from the Planet of the Cows.

My teenage sister, Tiffany, got pretty jealous of all the attention I was getting. When her class took a trip to the Air and Space Museum, she broke into the space rock exhibit and handled the same radioactive rocks that gave me my powers. It did give her superpowers, too, but she's a lousy superhero. I mean, she never really learned how to fly. She's always bumping into birds and buildings and stuff. Plus which she's not at all cool about having a secret identity. She keeps showing off and blowing her cover, and then I have to go find somebody to erase the memories of people who suspected she was a superhero. It's a real pain.

Anyway, back to saving the planet.

The way it started was that one day the seas got really rough. On both the East and West Coasts, the waves were higher than during a hurricane, only there wasn't any wind. Nobody could figure it out. Then the same thing started happening in other places, too. In Chicago, where I live, the waves on Lake Michigan were as high as a house. It was weird.

Then it got a whole lot weirder.

Just as we were about to sit down to dinner one Sunday evening, the President of the United States called me.

"Max," he said, "we have a situation in New York I need you to look into."

"What is it, sir?" I asked.

"Well, it seems some, uh . . . creatures have crawled out of the ocean and onto the beach in Brooklyn. On Coney Island."

"What kind of creatures?" I asked. "Sea turtles?"

"No, not exactly sea turtles," said the President. "These creatures are six or seven feet tall. They have scaly, armored plates instead of skin. They have long powerful tails. They look a little like people and a little like reptiles. Have you ever seen an old movie called *The Creature from the Black Lagoon?*"

"No, sir," I said.

"Too bad. Because they look a little like that. Have you seen the *Alien* movies? They look a little like the creatures in those movies, too."

"My mom wouldn't let me see those movies," I said. "She thought they were too scary for me."

"Mmm," said the President. "Anyway, Max, people on the beach in Coney Island panicked. They screamed and ran. The creatures didn't chase them. They just stood on the beach and waited. There are sixty or seventy of them, just waiting on the beach there now. Nobody knows what they're waiting for. You and Tiffany did such a great job with those nasty creatures from the Planet of the Cows. Could you guys fly out to Coney Island now and try to figure out what they want?"

"Has anybody tried to make contact with them?" I asked.

"No. Nobody's been brave enough to get close. And I don't think they're smart enough to speak. I'd really like you to fly out there now and check this out. Will your parents let you go?"

"I don't know, sir," I said. "I'll ask." I held my hand over the phone. "Mom and Dad," I said, "it's the President. It seems a bunch of creatures have crawled out of the ocean in Coney Island. The President wants me to find out what they are."

"But, Max, we're just about to sit down to dinner," said Mom.

"Uh-oh," said the President. "I've just been told that creatures like the ones in

Coney Island have crawled out of the water in California, too. In Malibu."

"Sir, Mom says we're just about to sit down to dinner," I said.

"We're having your favorite, Max," said Mom. "Pepperoni pizza."

"And you still have homework," said Dad. "You haven't finished that book report for school tomorrow."

"Uh-oh," said the President. "I've been told it's also happening in Southampton, England. And on the French Riviera. And in Acapulco, Mexico."

"Sir, we're having pepperoni pizza. And I haven't finished my book report for school tomorrow."

"Max, this is your President speaking. Your country needs you, son. It's your patriotic duty to go to Coney Island."

"Mom, Dad, the President says it's my patriotic duty to go to Coney Island."

Dad sighed. Mom shook her head.

"All right," said Mom. "If it's your patriotic duty, then I suppose you have to go. But take that book report with you. Maybe you'll find a quiet moment to work on it."

"Do I have to go, too?" said Tiffany.

"Does Tiffany have to go, too?" I asked the President.

"It's her patriotic duty," said the President.

"The President says it's your patriotic duty," I repeated.

"But flying will make my hair all yucky," said Tiffany.

"Sir, Tiffany says flying will make her hair all yucky."

"Son, those who serve their country are

often asked to make sacrifices. Sometimes those sacrifices include yucky hair."

"All right, sir. We're on our way," I said. I hung up the phone.

We thought all that was at stake was a book report and yucky hair. Little did we realize that what was really at stake were the lives of everybody on Earth.

CHAPTER 2

It took us almost an hour to fly to Coney Island. It shouldn't have taken that long, but Tiffany slowed us down. First, she had to stop for hair spray in Indiana. Then she had to stop for breath mints in Pennsylvania. Then she had to go to the bathroom in New Jersey. Finally, we got there.

From the air I could see all of Coney

Island. It's mostly this big amusement park, with tons of rides and an aquarium. There's a Ferris wheel and one of the oldest roller coasters in the world, the Cyclone. There's a boardwalk right next to the beach. The creatures were on the beach. There were sixty or seventy of them, easy. And they were really creepy looking. A little like alligators with short snouts and gills, and a little not.

On the boardwalk were about a dozen cop cars and vans with five or six film crews from the local TV channels. We flew down and landed next to a cop car. Tiffany looked at her reflection in the cop-car window.

"I knew it," she said. "Just look at my hair, Max. It's all yucky from flying."

"Hello there, Officer," I said. "I'm Maximum Boy. This is my sister, Maximum

Girl. The President of the United States has sent us to see what the creatures want. Got any ideas?"

"We sure don't," said the driver of the cop car. "They're just standing there, looking at us."

"How long have they been there like that?"

"Maybe an hour," said the cop. "We got a call about some alligators. Looks like a lot more than alligators. Boy, are they ever ugly."

"Probably *we* look ugly to *them*," I said.

"Good point," said the cop. "So tell me. How do you like being a superhero?"

"Oh, it's all right," I said. "But pretty tough on homework."

"And on hair," said Tiffany.

Suddenly, there was movement among the creatures. The biggest one took a step forward. He seemed to be their leader. Flaps extended all around his mouth, just like a megaphone. He began to speak. His voice was loud and kind of gurgly. It sounded like he was speaking through water.

"Grrreetings, Drrrylanderrrs!" he said. "We arrre the Waterrr People. We have come to take overrr yourrr worrrld."

"Uh-oh," said the cop. "That doesn't sound good."

"Who among you speaks forrr the Drrrylanderrrs?" asked the creature.

None of the cops or news reporters said a word.

"Who speaks forrr the Drrryland-errrs?!!" shouted the creature.

I realized it was probably me who had to answer. My heart started hammering in my chest. I was pretty scared, but I stepped forward. I could hardly breathe.

"*I* s-s-speak for the D-d-drylanders," I said.

"M-me too," said Tiffany, but so quietly not even the cops heard her.

The creature stretched its neck forward to look at me. Its neck extended at least five feet. Then it burst into horrible sounds that sounded like gurgly laughter. The other creatures started laughing, too.

"*You* speak forrr the Drrrylanderrrs?" roared the creature. "But you arrre only a *baby*."

That got me mad.

"A baby?" I said. "I am not a *baby*! I'm eleven and a half!"

The creature roared with more of its terrible laughter. So did the others. These things were not only ugly, they were rude. The creatures slowly got over their laughter.

"Since the little baby is the only

Drrrylanderrr brrrave enough to speak to us," it said, "I will speak to the little baby."

"Thanks a lot," I said sarcastically. "Thanks for *nothing*." I was pretty angry, but I remembered I was here on official business. "Where are you from, Atlantis?"

That started more nasty laughter.

"Atlantis is but a small parrrt of ourrr underrrwaterrr worrrld. Saying all Waterrr People arrre frrrom Atlantis is like saying all Drrrylanderrrs arrre frrrom Cleveland."

The creatures laughed some more.

"No, little baby, we arrre the Waterrr People. The Waterrr People live in all oceans, deep lakes, and rrriverrrs. Pitiful Drrrylanderrrs, this planet is ninety perrr-cent waterrr. We have generrrously al-lowed you to sharrre the planet, and what do you do? You pollute it. Yourrr tankerrr ships spill millions of gallons of oil into ourrr oceans. Yourrr factorrries spill toxic chemicals into ourrr rrriverrrs. When you go swimming, you pee in ourrr waterrr — in the waterrr we *brrreathe*. Well, we'rrre fed up and we'rrre not going to take it any longerrr!"

"Excuse me," I interrupted, "but Earth isn't ninety percent water, it's around seventy-five percent. We studied that in school."

"It *is* ninety perrrcent, little baby, if you include rrriverrrs, lakes, aquarrriums, swimming pools, and toilets. Who is the leaderrr of all the Drrrylanderrrs? I wish to speak to him."

"The leader of this particular country is

the President of the United States," I said.

"Then tell the Prrresident *this*, little baby: The Waterrr People have come to take overrr the Drrrylanderrrs and the Drrry Worrrld! Unless you surrrenderrr, we shall unleash upon all nations of the Drrry Worrrld devastating floods and tidal waves! We shall sink you! We shall drrrown you and drrrain you of your verrry last airrr bubble!"

"Yeah?" I said. "Well, we're not afraid of you."

"Pitiful Drrrylanderrrs!" shrieked the creature. "You are no match forrr the Waterrr People! We declarrre warrr on all Drrrylanderrrs, starrrting Thurrrsday! We wanted to make it Tuesday, but I had a dentist appointment."

"Thursday is fine with *us*!" I shouted.

OK, maybe I shouldn't have said that.

Maybe some people on Earth didn't want to go to war with the Water People. Or maybe they were busy on Thursday. I shouldn't have spoken for all the people on Earth without talking to the United Nations.

The President was going to be mad at me.

CHAPTER 3

"So how did it go in Coney Island?" asked the President.

Tiffany and I had flown right down to Washington to tell him what happened.

"Well, sir," I said, "to tell you the truth, it didn't go too well."

"What happened?"

"Sir, Max made a date with the Water People to go to war on Thursday," said Tiffany.

"Excuse me?" said the President.

"I did not," I said.

"Did too," said Tiffany.

"The *creature* said Thursday, Tiffany. All I said was 'fine.'"

"Would somebody please tell me what you're talking about here?" asked the President.

"OK," I said. "Sir, this is going to sound a lot worse than it is. But I kind of agreed that all the nations on Earth would go to war with the Water People on Thursday."

"You *what?*" said the President. His face got all red.

"I *know* I shouldn't have done that, OK?" I said. "I *know* you have to get permission from a whole lot of people before agreeing to a war. But he said they'd destroy Earth with floods and tidal waves, anyway, if we didn't surrender. Plus which he was calling me a little baby, and it really got me mad."

"Let me get this straight," said the President. His voice was really serious. "You have committed all the nations on Earth to a war with creatures from the ocean?"

"Not just the ocean, sir," I said. "They also count lakes, rivers, swimming pools, aquariums, and toilets. They're really scary, sir. They have these nasty-looking teeth and these gross-looking flaps that come out around their mouth when they speak. Our armed forces could probably blow them to bits in about ten minutes, couldn't they?"

The President didn't answer. He just stared at me, breathing hard. Then he picked up his phone.

"I want to see the Secretary of Defense

in my office," he said into the phone. "When? *Immediately*, that's when. I also want to call an emergency meeting of the United Nations. I want the top military leaders and the top scientists of all nations to be there. Is that all? No, that's not all. I also want you to get me a cheeseburger, a Dr Pepper, and a Snickers bar."

The next day was Monday. I don't know how he did it, but the President got his emergency meeting at the United Nations by three o'clock in the afternoon. Ambassadors from every country on Earth were there. And all the top military leaders from every nation. And all the top scientists, too. Tiffany and I asked if we could come, too. Even though he was still mad at me, the President said OK. He called our teachers and got us excused from school. It's lucky I didn't spend too much time on that book report.

The United Nations is in New York City. It's in this really nice little park, right on the East River. There's a tall, flat building with lots of glass called the Secretariat. There's a long, low building called the General Assembly. The meeting was in the General Assembly building, in a huge auditorium, bigger than the one at school.

The auditorium was crammed with people. They were dressed in suits and robes and strange-looking outfits. The press was there, too. Lots of TV cameras and TV lights. The President called the meeting to order.

"Thank you all for coming here on such short notice," said the President. "As you probably know by now, a hostile underwater nation called the Water People has declared war on us. They want the war to start on Thursday. They are threatening to destroy what they call the Dry World with floods and tidal waves unless we surrender."

"I say, who exactly are these Water People chaps?" asked the British ambassador. "I don't believe I've had the pleasure of meeting them."

"My people tell me they occupy ninety percent of the earth's surface," said the President.

I poked Tiffany. "Hey, the President just called us his *people*," I whispered.

"My word," said the British ambassador. "I thought Earth's surface was only *seventy-five* percent water."

"Well," said the President, "I believe

they're including lakes, rivers, swimming pools, aquariums, and toilets."

"Ah, quite so," said the British ambassador. "But the Water People chaps aren't members of the United Nations, are they?"

"No," said the President.

"Well, then," said the British ambassador, "I daresay we can't go to war with them. I vote no."

"I'm afraid it's not up for a vote," said the President. "The Water People have declared war on us. We must do something and do it fast."

"I think we should drop a bunch of atomic bombs into the ocean and blast them out of the water," said an American admiral.

A lot of people thought that was a great idea, mostly military ones.

"No, no!" said a French scientist. "Eef we

do thees, we weel also destroy all life on dry land as we know eet!"

"Heck, what's wrong with that?" said the admiral.

The scientist rolled his eyes and muttered something in French.

"I have an idea," said the Canadian ambassador. "Why should so many people die? Why don't we have the strongest person on dry land fight the strongest person in the underwater world? We'll have three physical contests. If our guy wins two of the three, then we Drylanders win the war. The Water People will go back underwater and promise never to bother us again."

"But what if *their* guy wins?" said the Australian ambassador. "What do we do *then*, mate — just lie down and let them take over our countries?"

Everybody in the place started yelling at once. The President rapped for order. It took a while for everyone to get quiet again.

"Their guy will *not* win," said the President.

"How can you be sure, mate?" said the Australian ambassador.

"Because," said the President, "we'll make sure that whoever we choose to represent us is stronger than whoever *they* choose. In fact, among our honored guests today are several members of the League of Superheroes."

This was news to me. A lot of people in the audience applauded when they heard that. I looked over the audience to see what superheroes were here.

The President was right. There was Iron Man, who was about eight feet tall. He had a chest of iron plates welded together and fists made out of iron spikes. A few seats away was Garbage Man. He compacted his enemies like a giant trash compactor. In the next row was Elastic Woman, who could wrap herself around somebody's neck like a snake and choke them. Coiled up in her lap was Noodleman, who usually hangs out in bowls of spaghetti.

On the aisle were my old friends, Tortoise Man and his wife, Tortoise Woman. Tortoise Man was one of the slowest people on Earth but a really sweet guy. Both he and his wife were pretty much retired by now, but I was glad they were here.

"I'm told that the strongest of the superheroes is Iron Man," said the President. "Iron Man, would you please stand up?"

Iron Man stood up. There were loud

creaking noises as he stood. When people saw how big he was, they burst into applause again.

"With all of your permission," said the President, "I'd like to appoint Iron Man to represent the Drylanders."

Everybody started cheering like crazy.

"Iron Man is a pretty good choice," said Tiffany over the cheering.

"Yeah," I said. "I don't think he's ever lost a fight."

The cheers became chants of "*I*-ron Man! *I*-ron Man! If *he* can't do it, *no* one can!"

Finally, Iron Man held up one of his huge, spiked fists for quiet. When the crowd calmed down, he spoke. His voice was very deep and kind of hoarse.

"Mr. President," rasped Iron Man. "Thank you for the honor of choosing me to

fight for all the people on Earth. But I'm afraid I have to say no. You see, I just came down with a very bad case of rust."

Everybody in the audience groaned. You could see they'd been really counting on Iron Man. Iron Man sat down again, creaking even louder than before.

"All right," said the President. "That's too bad. I was really counting on Iron Man to defend us. But we have other superheroes here. Like Garbage Man. Garbage Man, would you like to defend Earth from the Water People?"

Garbage Man got to his feet. He was wearing white coveralls, rubber gloves, and boots.

"Mr. President," said Garbage Man. "First of all, a correction. I've changed my name to Sanitation Man. And, sir, I'm as honored as Iron Man to be asked to defend the people of Earth. But the thing of it is, I'm right in the middle of seriously cleaning up my act. If you could put this off for a few weeks, maybe I could do it. But not now."

There were groans from the audience.

"Frankly," said the President, "I doubt that the Water People are going to agree to wait a few weeks to start their war. But we have other superheroes. Like Elastic Woman. Elastic Woman, do you think you could handle this?"

Elastic Woman was wearing a pink leotard. She stayed seated but stretched her head and neck up high enough to be seen by everybody.

"Mr. President," said Elastic Woman, "I'm also honored to be asked to defend the people of Earth. But, like Sanitation Man and Iron Man, I'm afraid I also have to say no. I've been pretty stretched out lately. I'm saggy and I've lost a lot of my snap."

There were more groans.

"All right," said the President. "Who else have we got?"

"What about Noodleman?" said Elastic Woman.

"As much as I like Noodleman personally," said the President, "I just don't think that a foot-long piece of talking spaghetti is going to be able to save the people of Earth."

There was a lot of shouting from the audience. The President somehow managed to get everybody quiet again.

"My good friend Maximum Boy is with us today," said the President. "He's only eleven, but he's beaten a lot of nasty supervillains. Plus which, he's already had contact with the Water People in Coney Island. What about it, Maximum Boy? Do you think you could defend Earth against the Water People?"

Everybody turned around to look at me. Oh, boy, did that make me nervous!

I stood up and cleared my throat.

"M-mister President," I said. "Like Iron Man, Sanitation Man, and Elastic Woman, I'm also real honored and stuff. But as you said, I'm only eleven. And I have a whole lot of homework besides. And, to tell you the truth, I really hate putting my face in the water. So I don't see how I could fight these guys."

More groans from the audience. You could tell they were getting depressed.

"I'd like to point out, Maximum Boy," said the President, "that when the evil Dr.

Zirkon towed the island of Manhattan out to sea, it was you who got it back for us. You beat both Dr. Zirkon and his sidekick, Nobblock, underwater. And they were wearing scuba suits."

"That's true, sir," I said.

Everybody applauded.

"You even beat a giant octopus," said the President.

Everybody applauded again.

"How many of you think Maximum Boy could defeat the Water People?" yelled the President.

Everybody started cheering. It got louder and louder.

"Maximum Boy!" yelled the President over the cheering. "All the people of Earth need you to defend us! You must accept this challenge! It's your patriotic duty!"

"Tiffany," I yelled over the cheering. "What should I do?"

"Tell them you'll do it," she said.

"But I hate putting my face in the water," I said.

"So, wear nose plugs," she said.

I sighed and held up both my arms for quiet.

So did the President. People got quiet again.

"All right, sir," I said. "If you want me that bad, I'll do it."

Everybody in the whole United Nations went absolutely crazy.

Great. So if I won, I'd be this huge hero. And if I lost, everybody on Earth would drown, including me. It wasn't fair. I mean, it really wasn't fair.

CHAPTER 4

Mom and Dad met me at the door.

"So what happened today at the UN?" asked my dad.

"Are we going to war with the Water People on Thursday or not?" asked my mom.

"Well," I said, "there's good news and bad news. The good news is, there isn't going to be a regular war."

"That's marvelous!" said my mom. "I really don't like wars very much."

"That's absolutely great!" said my dad. "What's the *bad* news?"

"The bad news," I said, "is that one person on Earth is going to battle one person from the Water People. And whoever wins will win the war. And the person defending Earth is me."

Mom and Dad looked like somebody had punched them in the stomach.

"This is terrible," said Mom. "You know how allergic you are to water, dear. You don't even like to put your face in it."

"I know that, Mom," I said.

"He'll get swimmer's ear," she said to my dad. "And *then* what?" She began to cry.

"Son, how long can you hold your breath underwater?" asked my dad.

"About a minute," I said.

"About a minute," my dad repeated. "How can you possibly fight Water People underwater if you can only hold your breath for a minute?"

"I don't know, Dad," I said. "I guess I'll practice holding my breath in the bathtub. The war isn't till Thursday. Maybe I'll improve."

CHAPTER 5

The next day was Tuesday. As soon as I got to school, my teacher took me aside.

"Max, what happened yesterday at the UN?" she asked.

"Well, Mrs. Mulvahill," I said, "the war with the Water People starts Thursday. They want me to defend Earth."

"Oh, my," she said.

"I know," I said. "It's a lot of responsibility."

"That's not what I meant," she said. "I meant you'll be missing school again. And Thursday is the day of the sixth-grade midterm exams."

"Mrs. Mulvahill, I may get *killed* on Thursday. And all you're worried about is that I'll be missing school and some stupid exams?"

"I'm sorry, Max. Of *course* I'm worried about your safety. But you always do so well as a superhero, I just assume you'll be all right. The problem is that you've missed so much school. If you miss the midterms, I'm afraid you may have to repeat the sixth grade."

"What?"

"Yes, Max. The school principal, Mr.

Stinkerton, is very concerned about how much school you've been missing. He says if you miss any more, I'll have to flunk you."

"But it's not my fault! The President keeps sending me out on all these missions. Doesn't Mr. Stinkerton know that?"

"I'm the only one at this school who knows your secret identity. You told me never to tell anyone."

"But is it fair to flunk me for trying to save the people of Earth?"

"No, no. Of course not. Look, Max, I'll talk to Mr. Stinkerton about this. Maybe I can get him to change his mind."

I couldn't concentrate all morning in class. I kept thinking how unfair it was that trying to save my country might make me flunk the sixth grade. I kept thinking about the creature I was going to have to fight on Thursday.

My teacher was worried about my missing school. My mom and dad were worried about my getting swimmer's ear. Why wasn't anybody worried about an eight-foot-tall monster tearing me to pieces? I mean, it's true I have superpowers, but I'm still just an eleven-year-old boy with glasses, braces, and allergies.

I'd seen what these creatures looked like on the beach at Coney Island. How was I going to win against something like that?

And what if I lost? I'd probably drown. Worse yet, I'd be responsible for every human being on Earth drowning, too. I couldn't stand it. It was too much. I put my head down on my desk. I was really depressed.

"Max," said Mrs. Mulvahill, "are you feeling ill?"

"A little," I said.

"Would you like to go downstairs and see the school nurse?"

"No, that's OK," I said.

"Please go down and see the school nurse," said Mrs. Mulvahill.

I sighed and got up from my desk. I went downstairs to the infirmary.

The school nurse was wearing a white uniform and a little white nurse's cap.

"Can I help you?" she asked.

"Mrs. Mulvahill told me to come down and see you."

"What seems to be the trouble?"

"Nothing you could help me with."

"Are you feeling sick?"

"Not really," I said. "I guess I might be a little, you know, depressed."

"Are you worried about something?"

"Yeah, I guess I am."

"What are you worried about?"

"I, uh, can't really tell you that."

"Why can't you tell me what you're worried about?" she asked.

"It's . . . kind of complicated," I said.

"Is it something at school? Or at home?"

"Neither one."

"Well, whatever you're worrying about, I'm sure you're making it out to be a lot more than it actually is."

"I don't think so," I said.

"Well," she said with a little chuckle, "it's not like it's the end of the *world*, you know."

"No," I said. "Actually, it *is*."

The nurse squeezed my hand again. I went back to my class.

At lunch my best friend, Charlie Sparks, came racing over to me. She's real little, but she's tougher than lots of guys I know. She's the only kid my age who knows I'm Maximum Boy. She's the only one I trust. You could pull out Charlie's fingernails and she'd never tell.

"Max," she said, "what happened at the UN?"

"Ssshhh," I said, looking around to see if anybody had heard her. Nobody had. "OK, the people at the UN chose me to defend Earth," I said. "I have to battle the strongest of the Water People on Thursday."

"Oh, wow, that's so cool. Are you scared?"

"Uh, no, not really," I said.

"If it was me," said Charlie, "I'd be peeing in my pants."

"OK," I said. "If you want to know the truth, Charlie, I *am* a little nervous."

"What are you nervous about, Silver?" asked a familiar voice in back of me.

I turned around. It was Trevor Fartmeister, the school bully! A kid so scary, nobody ever makes jokes about his name. Fartmeister has a red buzz cut and half his left ear is missing. I heard a kid even bigger than Fartmeister bit it off in a fight. I heard Fartmeister bit off the other kid's nose.

"I said, what are you nervous about?" Fartmeister repeated.

"A test in school," I said.

"In what subject?"

"Math."

"Yeah? I heard you're *allergic* to math," said Fartmeister. "I heard you got a doctor's *excuse* to get out of math."

"So?"

"So if you got a doctor's excuse to get out of math, then you don't got to take no *test* in it. In which case you're lying to me. Are you lying to me, Silver?"

A bunch of kids came over to watch. The kids in my school love to see other kids get picked on. I think they're just glad it isn't them.

"OK, I'm lying to you," I said.

"You're the first person that's ever had the guts to lie to me. So you get a prize."

"What do I get?"

"Half of my sardine and liverwurst sandwich."

"Thanks, but I brought my own lunch."

"My *mother* made this sandwich for me, Silver. Are you insulting my mother by refusing to eat the sandwich she made?"

"Uh, well, no. OK, give me the sandwich."

He handed me half his sandwich. I really don't like sardines or liverwurst. I couldn't even imagine how gross they'd taste together. But I didn't want to fight with him. I mean, with my superpowers I could crush him like a bug. But that would blow my cover and it would put my mom and dad in danger. I took a bite of the sandwich.

Fartmeister burst out laughing.

"I spit on that sandwich before I gave it to you," he said.

I gagged and spit out what was in my mouth. The other kids laughed.

"Ha-ha, just kidding," said Fartmeister.

"I didn't spit on it before I gave it to you. But I will *now*." He grabbed the sandwich and spat on it. "Go ahead, Silver," he said. "Eat it."

"No way," I said.

"Eat it or I'll shove it down your throat," he said.

"Why don't you leave him alone?" said Charlie.

"Why don't you make me?" said Fartmeister.

"Whatever you say," said Charlie.

She punched Fartmeister in the belly. His eyes bugged out and he almost fell down.

Then he burst out laughing. Fartmeister is about three times as big as Charlie. I told you she was tough.

"You're a piece of work, kid, you know that?" said Fartmeister. "I'd hit you back, but then everybody would say I was hitting a little girl."

"You're right," said Charlie.

"So I ain't gonna hit you," said Fartmeister.

"Good," said Charlie.

"Because I got a better idea," said Fartmeister.

He picked Charlie up by the back of her shirt. He carried her to a huge open trash can and started to throw her in. I couldn't let him do that to my best friend. But I couldn't use my superpowers and blow my cover, either. I went up to him and stomped hard on his foot.

He dropped Charlie and came for me.

"Now you've done it, Silver," he growled. "Now you've really done it. I try and be nice to you. I try to give you half a sandwich my mother made me. And how do you thank me? You stomp on my foot. You know what I'm going to do to you, Silver?"

Trevor Fartmeister was going to kill me. I didn't know what to do. Then I remembered a story from when I was little. A fox catches a rabbit and is going to eat him, but

the rabbit outsmarts him. He tells the fox he can do whatever he wants to him, just so long as he doesn't throw him in the briar patch. The fox throws him in the briar patch. But the briar patch is where the rabbit lives, and he scampers away, laughing.

"I don't care what you do to me, Fartmeister," I said. "Just please don't punch me in the stomach."

"Why not?"

"Because that's how Harry Houdini, the magician, got killed. Somebody punched him in the stomach. So do whatever you like to me, but please, *please* don't punch me in the stomach."

With a nasty laugh, Fartmeister raised his fist and punched me in the stomach with all his might. Just before his fist hit me, I used my superpowers to make my stomach as hard as a rock.

Trevor Fartmeister shouted with pain. He started dancing around, holding his hurt fist. The kids laughed. Charlie cheered.

"You broke my hand!" cried Fartmeister. "What the heck you got in there, a steel plate?"

"That's exactly what it is," I said. "A steel plate. I put it in there just before lunch, in case I ran into you."

CHAPTER 6

By the end of the day on Tuesday, Mrs. Mulvahill still hadn't been able to talk to Mr. Stinkerton about my missing school on Thursday. But I felt so great about beating Trevor Fartmeister, I wasn't too upset.

When I took my bath, Dad timed me holding my breath underwater. I tried several times and finally got my time up to a minute and a half.

"You're going to have to do lots better than a minute and a half, son, if you're going to fight the Underwater People," said my dad.

"I know that, Dad," I said.

The next day when I got to class, Mrs. Mulvahill took me aside.

"I spoke to Mr. Stinkerton," she said.

"What did he say?"

"Well, I told him you needed to be out of school on Thursday. At first, he was quite upset that you wouldn't be able to take the sixth-grade midterm exams. He wanted me to flunk you. But then I told him you really needed to be gone. He asked why, but I wouldn't tell him. He finally agreed to a compromise."

"What's that?"

"He's going to allow you to miss school on Thursday without flunking you. Provided that you still take the midterm exams."

"But how can I do that? I'm going to be fighting the Water People and trying to save all the people of Earth."

"Well, he's sending Irwin Pukebreath, our new assistant principal, to go with you.

He'll be giving you the midterm exams while you're fighting."

"You're kidding me, right?"

"No, Max, I'm quite serious."

"Does Mr. Pukebreath know I'm Maximum Boy?"

"I'm afraid I'll have to tell him. I mean, once he sees you in your outfit, flying around battling the Water People, he'll probably guess, anyway."

CHAPTER 7

The dreaded Thursday finally came.

I was supposed to meet the Water Person I was going to fight on the beach at Coney Island at six a.m. I guess the Water People are early risers. I'm not at all a morning person, so meeting anybody that early, especially an eight-foot monster, was kind of a problem for me.

It was pretty chilly. The sun was just

about to come up. The sky was pink in the east. You could see the Ferris wheel and the steep hills of the Cyclone roller coaster in the background. The ocean was very flat, with only the smallest of waves lapping the shore.

The beach and the boardwalk were jammed. Around seventy or eighty crocodile-like Water People stood without moving. There were tons of film crews from TV stations all over the world. There were lots of cops and soldiers. I didn't know why they needed soldiers since I was going to be the only one fighting.

They had set up stands on the board-walk for people to watch. My mom and dad were there. So was Tiffany in her Maximum Girl outfit. There were already several hundred people seated there, waiting for the battle to start. Waiting to see me get killed by a monster. I was pretty scared. I felt like any second I was going to puke my guts out.

Then somebody tapped me on the shoulder. I turned around.

"Tortoise Man!" I said. "Boy, am I ever glad to see *you*! What are you doing here?"

"I came to cheer for you, the same as everybody else," said Tortoise Man.

"Listen," I said. "You're a sea creature. Have you ever run into any of the Water People before?"

"Years ago, when I was very young," he said. "I went fishing with them. They're pretty nasty, I have to tell you. They ate my bait."

The Secretary General of the United Nations came up to me.

"Maximum Boy," he said, "all the

nations of Earth are grateful for what you are doing here today."

"Thanks," I said. "Has anybody spoken to the Water People about the terms of the battle?"

He nodded.

"I have personally spoken to the leader of the Water People," he said. "His name is Chortle. He's quite unpleasant, by the way. And he smells like rotting fish. He agreed that a battle between the strongest members of both sides was better than a war involving thousands of soldiers."

"Yeah, right," I said. "He knows our navy would blow them right out of the water. Did he agree to our terms?"

"Yes," said the Secretary General. "There will be three challenges. Whoever wins a coin toss will present the first challenge. Whoever wins the first challenge will present the second challenge, and so on. The first competitor to win two challenges wins the war."

A tall, bald guy wearing steel-rimmed glasses came up to me.

"Good morning," he said. "My name is Irwin Pukebreath. I'm the assistant principal of your school. Mr. Stinkerton sent me to give you the sixth-grade midterm examination."

I remembered seeing him at school. Except I didn't remember his butt being so big.

"Listen, Mr. Pukebreath," I said. "I'm so nervous, I'm ready to throw up myself."

"I quite understand," he said. "The sixth-grade midterms are quite difficult."

"That's not what's making me nauseous,"

I said. "It's the other thing I have to do today."

"You have something else to do today besides the sixth-grade midterms?"

"They didn't tell you?" I said.

He shook his head.

"I was merely told you would meet me at dawn on the beach at Coney Island, and that the exams would be given there. What else do you have to do besides take the exam?"

"I'm trying to defend the people of Earth from monsters who want to wipe us all out," I said.

"I see," said Pukebreath. "And how long do you estimate this will take?"

Just then, Chortle, the leader of the Water People, made a loud noise. The flaps came out around his mouth and he began to speak.

"Drrrylanderrrs!" Chortle bellowed. "Yourrr last day of frrreedom has arrrived! Prrreparrre to meet yourrr conquerrrorrr! At the moment of sunrrrise, I shall intrrroduce the mighty Gorrrgle. Gorrrgle is the grrreatest and most fearrrsome of all the Waterrr People. It is he who will battle yourrr pitiful rrreprrresentative to the death!"

Oh, boy, did I ever not like the sound of *that*! I was feeling so nauseous, I would have thrown up my entire breakfast. Except for the fact I had been too nauseous to *eat* breakfast.

I looked at the sky. Just at the ocean's horizon line, the very top of an orange sun began to appear. Suddenly, there was turbulence in the calm ocean. The waters seemed to boil. Then, out of the middle of the turbulence burst the worst-looking thing I have ever seen in my life.

The people in the stands gasped. The thing that came out of the ocean looked like a Water Person, only bigger and uglier. It must have stood at least ten feet tall. It had long, webbed claws. It had rows of nasty-looking teeth. It had jagged armored plates along its back and a long powerful tail. It was greenish black, and it dripped slime.

"Pitiful Drrrylanderrrs," said Chortle, "may I prrresent yourrr worrrst nightmarrre . . . the one, the only . . . Gorrrgle!"

Everybody booed except the Water People on the beach. They trumpeted and stomped the ground with their webbed feet till the sand shook.

"And now," said Chortle, "who rrreprrresents the Drrrylanderrrs? Step forrrwarrrd so that Gorrrgle may see whom he is going to defeat!"

My knees were shaking so badly I could hardly walk.

The crowd in the stands began to cheer. They started chanting, "Max-i-mum Boy, Max-i-mum Boy! Crush the Wa-ter Per-son like a toy!"

I stepped forward.

Chortle burst out laughing.

"You?" he shrieked. "*You* will defend the Drrrylanderrrs? Does the tiny little baby think he can crrrush the mighty Gorrrgle?"

Then all the Water People started laughing, too.

"Shut up!" I shouted. "I'll kick Gorgle's butt! And when I'm done I'll kick yours, too!"

Somebody tapped me on the shoulder. It was Pukebreath.

"All right," said Pukebreath. "Here's your first question."

"Not now, Pukebreath," I said. "Can't you see I'm busy?"

"That's *Mister* Pukebreath," said Pukebreath. "And the question is: "What river forms a boundary between Mexico and the United States? Is it (A) the Mississippi, (B) the Rio Grande, or (C) the Amazon?"

"The Rio Grande," I said. "Now will you please leave me alone?"

"Who is the baby Drrrylanderrr speaking to?" Chortle asked.

"The Rio Grande is correct," said Pukebreath. "Your next question is —"

"I said not *now*, Mr. Pukebreath!"

"— what body of water lies between Mexico and the Atlantic? Is it (A) the Caribbean, (B) the Congo, or (C) the Gulf of Mexico?"

"It's the Gulf of Mexico, but I —"

"Is the Drrrylanderrr baby going to listen to me?" shrieked Chortle. "Orrr is he going to forrrfeit the entirrre match rrright now?"

"I'm *listening*, I'm *listening*!" I shouted.

"The Gulf of Mexico is correct," said Puke-breath.

"I shall now flip a coin," said Chortle. "You shall call it in the airrr. Whoeverrr wins will choose the firrrst challenge."

Chortle tossed a coin in the air.

"Heads!" shouted Gorgle.

"Tails!" I yelled. Everybody looked at me. I felt really stupid.

Chortle picked up the coin and looked at it.

"It is heads," he said. "Gorrrgle will now choose the firrrst challenge."

"Do you mind if I take a look at that coin?" I asked, but nobody heard me.

"Firrrst challenge," said Gorgle. "Rrraise the sunken Drrrylanderrr ship the *Titanic*. Firrrst, Gorrrgle will do it. Then *you* can trrry. Gorrrgle will swim to the *Titanic*. How will *you* get therrre, little baby?"

"Fly," I said.

Gorgle dove into the water and started swimming so fast he looked like a speedboat.

"All right, Maximum Boy," said Pukebreath, "your next question is —"

"Look, Mr. Pukebreath," I said, "I'm trying to defend the people of Earth from destruction here. If you distract me, I'm going to lose. And then you and I and everybody on Earth are going to drown. Do you understand me?"

"*Your* job is to defend Earth," said Pukebreath. "*My* job is to give you the sixth-grade test. You do *your* job and I'll do *mine*. Now please name the body of water that lies north of Canada. Is it —"

"The Arctic Ocean," I said.

"Please," said Pukebreath. "You did not let me give you the three choices. Is it (A) the Arctic Ocean, (B) the *Ant*arctic Ocean, or —"

"The Arctic Ocean," I said.

"— or (C) the Indian Ocean?"

"The Arctic Ocean," I said.

"The Arctic Ocean is correct," said Pukebreath.

"See you later," I said and leaped into the air.

"I'll be here with your next question when you return!" he called after me.

CHAPTER 8

As I flew over the waves of the Atlantic Ocean, I could clearly see Gorgle swimming several yards below the surface. He was going so fast, he left a wake. Behind me flew about a dozen helicopters. One was a United Nations helicopter, which held the Secretary General of the UN and Chortle. The others were all probably TV film crews.

The *Titanic* was a British ocean liner

that hit an iceberg and sank in the North Atlantic on April 14, 1912. Out of the 2,200 passengers on board, 1,500 lost their lives. Lots of people know where the *Titanic* lies, but so far nobody has been able to raise it to the surface.

I didn't know how strong this Gorgle character was. I frankly didn't know if I was strong enough to raise it myself. But I couldn't let Gorgle beat me. I just couldn't.

The sun was a lot higher in the sky by the time we got to the *Titanic*. I saw Gorgle dive. I switched on my laser vision and watched him swim down to the wreck. I could see it way on the bottom, all brown and rusting away. It was in two pieces. Gorgle swam twice around the ship, probably trying to figure the best place to try and lift it from. Then he disappeared underneath it.

I flew in large circles over the place where the *Titanic* sank. So far, no sight of Gorgle. The longer it took, the better it was for me. Maybe Gorgle wouldn't be able to do it. I sure didn't want to go way down there and try to raise the *Titanic* myself. The longest I could hold my breath was about ninety seconds. Using my superpowers, I could probably get down to the wreck in thirty seconds.

If I could come back up again in another thirty seconds, what's the longest I could spend getting a grip under the ship? I tried to figure it out and felt myself starting to get dizzy. No! I couldn't even *try* to do math problems in my head. I couldn't risk going unconscious.

The helicopters hovered overhead. Still no Gorgle. What happened to him? Did he drown? No, he was a Water Person. He *breathed* water. Just as I was beginning to have hope Gorgle wasn't strong enough to lift an ocean liner, I saw something. The *Titanic*. It was slowly starting to rise.

My heart sank. It looked like Gorgle was going to do it after all. Then it would be *my* turn. Sure enough, in another minute or so the smokestacks of the *Titanic* broke the surface of the water. Then the bigger part of the cracked ship was above water. Yucky brown junk hung from every part of it. It was brown with rust and looked like it was going to fall apart any second.

Gorgle came out from underneath the ship and waved at the helicopters. I guess he wanted to make sure they saw he had really done it. Then he let go. The ship began to sink immediately. In a few seconds it was gone again.

Now it was *my* turn. I didn't think I could do it, I really didn't. I had a very bad feeling about this. *Well*, I thought, *here goes nothing*. I took a really deep breath, and then, holding my nose with one hand, I dove.

I hadn't descended more than a hundred feet when I saw something I never wanted to see. *Several* somethings, in fact. Sharks! A whole school of sharks were swimming toward me as fast as they could!

We studied sharks in the sixth grade. Sharks have been around a really long time. Did you know that sharks were swimming in the ocean 200 million years before dinosaurs? Well, they were.

Sharks have this really awesome sense of smell. Some sharks can see in almost total darkness. Some sharks bite with a pressure of 16,000 pounds per square inch. But the crushing power of their jaws is nothing compared to the sharpness of their teeth. When a shark bites you, it shakes its head from side to side. Its razor-sharp teeth will sink through your body like it's a Mallomar.

Sharks don't normally bite humans. Sharks only bite humans by mistake, when they confuse us with something they usually eat, like seals or fish. Well, I don't know what these guys thought I was, because they were coming straight for me, with their mouths wide open!

Sharks are incredibly sensitive to low-frequency sounds and to magnetic fields. That's how they find their way through the oceans without getting lost. It's also how they find their prey. All their radar equipment is in their noses, which means their noses are their most vulnerable parts.

As the first shark reached me, I punched him hard in the nose. He swam away fast. I punched the second shark in the nose. And the third. The sharks scattered, but now I was out of air. I swam toward the surface as fast as I could. My lungs were bursting without air. I was beginning to get dizzy. Just as I thought I was going to drown, my head broke the surface. I gulped air hungrily. Boy, was I glad to be able to breathe again!

The helicopters were still hovering overhead. They could see that I hadn't yet raised
the *Titanic*. They obviously knew I was having trouble. They knew that their fate — and
the fate of every human on Earth — was in
my hands. I couldn't let them down, I just
couldn't. I took another deep breath of air,
and I dove again.

This time I got within fifty yards of the wreck. It was gigantic. I only had a few seconds to figure out how to do this. I swam around the ship's bottom, looking for something to grab onto.

That's when I saw it. A whale as big as an apartment building. I mean, it was tremendous. Whales are very gentle and almost never attack humans. I guess this whale hadn't heard about that. He opened his jaws. Before I could figure out where to punch him, he swallowed me whole!

CHAPTER 9

I don't know if you've ever been inside of a whale, but it's dark, wet, and slimy. When you first come in, there's this huge area like the lobby of a hotel. That's the mouth.

Right after that, you go down this tunnel like a slide in a water park. That's the throat, or esophagus. When you get to the stomach, there's all kinds of stuff sloshing around in there. Tons of fish and stuff. And stomach acid to digest the food. It stinks, but the main thing is, at least there's enough air to breathe for a while.

So I sat in the whale's stomach and breathed for a while and tried to figure out what to do next. I knew I could always punch my way out of there if I had to. Use my superpowers to become a human drill and burrow my way out. But I didn't want to hurt the whale if I could help it.

Then I realized I could probably get out the same way I got in. It was slippery as anything, but I made my way out of the stomach back to the esophagus, and I carefully crawled back up to the mouth. I hung around in the mouth for a while and waited till the whale opened it. Then I snuck out.

By the time I reached the surface again, I was in pretty bad shape. Water had gone

up my nose and into my ears. I'd swallowed
a lot of it. Because it was ocean water, it was
pretty salty. I barfed all over the place. I
knew I didn't have it in me to go back down
to the floor of the ocean again and take
another shot at lifting the *Titanic*.

"All rrright, little baby, time is up!"

boomed a voice from overhead. There was a public-address system on the UN helicopter, and Chortle was talking to me. "Gorrrgle has rrraised the *Titanic*, and you have not! He wins rrround one! This means the Mighty Gorrrgle has won the rrright to choose the challenge forrr rrround two!"

Oh, no. If Gorgle won the first round, I had to win both of the next two, or I'd lose the war!

"We shall now rrreturrrn to Coney Island to begin rrround two!"

CHAPTER 10

"So how did it go with the *Titanic*?" asked Tortoise Man as soon as I got back to Coney Island.

"Not too good," I said. "I got attacked by sharks and swallowed by a whale, and then I got water up my nose. Gorgle won."

"Oh, my," said Tortoise Man. "Well, I'm sure you'll do better in round two. How are you feeling? You don't look too good."

"I'm OK," I said, but I really wasn't.

"Ah, there you are," said Pukebreath. "Let us continue the midterm exams."

"I have a better idea," I said. "Let's not."

"What atoms make up a molecule of water?" Pukebreath asked.

"I don't have time for this now, Mr. Pukebreath," I said.

"You do until the helicopters return."

"All right, all right," I said. "What atoms make up a molecule of water? Let me see. OK, one of hydrogen and two of oxygen. No, wait. Two of hydrogen and one of oxygen. No . . . I'm sorry. I'm just too nervous to remember."

"Too bad. Next: What is the only metal that flows at room temperature?"

Just then, we heard the helicopters

returning. Their engines were very loud.

"They're back," I said over the noise.

"What is the only metal that flows at room temperature?" Pukebreath shouted.

"Mercury?" I yelled.

"Correct!" Pukebreath shouted.

The helicopters landed.

"Attention, pitiful Drrrylanderrrs!" Chortle announced on the public-address system. His voice echoed all over Coney Island. "The mighty Gorrrgle has won the firrrst event, as he shall soon win them all! The scorrre is now Waterrr People one, Drrrylanderrrs zerrro!"

The creatures on the beach went crazy, trumpeting and smacking the sand. The people in the stands were very quiet.

There was a sudden turbulence in the

still waters of the ocean, and then Gorgle shot up onto the beach. The creatures went crazy again.

"Who is the mightiest crrreaturrre on land orrr waterrr?" shouted Chortle.

"Gorrrgle!" shrieked the creatures on the beach.

"Who?" shouted Chortle.

"Gorrrgle!" shrieked the creatures on the beach even louder.

"I cannot *hearrr* you!" shouted Chortle.

"Gorrrgle!" shrieked the creatures on the beach so loudly I had to hold my ears.

"Hey!" I yelled. "Can we skip the cheer-leading and just get on with the war?"

Nobody seemed to be paying any attention to me at all.

"Now Gorrrgle shall announce the second challenge!" shouted Chortle.

Gorgle walked onto the sand. Flaps like Chortle's shot out all around his mouth, making a megaphone.

"Second challenge!" shouted Gorgle. "Gorrrgle will take the Statue of Liberrrty and move it to its rrrightful place in the underrrwaterrr kingdom!"

"What?" I yelled. "That's not a challenge, that's stealing a national monument!"

"Baby Drrrylanderrr will be frrree to trrry and stop Gorrrgle if he can!" said Chortle.

With that, Gorgle dove into the water and sped away.

"Max, this is terrible!" said Tortoise Man. "You have to stop him!"

I leaped into the air.

"I'm on my way!" I yelled down to him.

The people in the stands waved to me and cheered, but I knew they were pretty worried. If I couldn't stop Gorgle from stealing the Statue of Liberty, the war would be over and we'd lose everything.

CHAPTER 11

I don't know how he did it. But by the time I flew to the Statue of Liberty in New York Harbor, Gorgle was already climbing out of the water.

"Don't do it, Gorgle!" I yelled. "The Statue of Liberty is United States Government property. Stealing it is a felony and a federal crime!"

In answer, Gorgle walked up the base of

the statue and began pushing against it as hard as he could. I heard a low, cracking sound.

"OK, Gorgle," I said. "Stop now or I'm going to really kick your butt!"

That was a bluff. I wasn't at all sure I *could* kick Gorgle's butt. To tell you the truth, I wasn't even sure Gorgle *had* a butt.

Gorgle acted like he hadn't even heard me. Having made a cracking sound by pushing the bottom of the statue as hard as he could, he started pulling it toward him. I heard another low, cracking sound. If he kept this up, he was going to crack the statue right off its base.

I heard a flupp-flupp-flupping sound, and the helicopters appeared overhead.

"OK, Gorgle!" I said. "That's it!"

I charged Gorgle at superspeed. I hit

him in the back as hard as I could. He spun around and kicked me in the belly. That caught me by surprise and knocked the wind out of me. I gasped for breath and stumbled backward. When Fartmeister hit me in the stomach, I was expecting it. This time I wasn't. I fell down and couldn't breathe.

Gorgle pushed the statue as hard as he could. There was an even louder cracking sound. The Statue of Liberty came off its base. Gorgle started dragging it toward the water.

"Ho-ho!" said Chortle over the loudspeaker on the UN helicopter. "The mighty Gorrrgle is about to beat the little Drrrylanderrr baby and win the entirrre warrr!"

Boy, did that ever make me mad!

I struggled to sit up. I somehow stood up. I flew at Gorgle with all my might. But I was so weak I landed short, right on the end of his tail. Without even knowing what I was doing, I bit his tail. Hard.

Gorgle screamed in surprise. He tried to whip his tail out of my mouth. I held on tight with superstrength.

"Let go!" he shrieked.

"*Grrrr!*" was all I could say with his tail in my mouth.

"That *hurrrts* Gorrrgle!" he whined.

"*Grrrr!*" I bit off the end of his tail.

"*Arrrggghhh!*" said Gorgle and let go of the statue.

I spit out his tail and caught the statue in superspeed before it hit the water. I flew it back to its base. Then I used my laser eyesight to melt the rock and fuse it in place.

I looked back at Gorgle. He was on the

sand on his hands and knees, searching for the end of his tail.

"The Statue of Liberty has been saved!" I shouted. "Round two is over and I win!"

"The tiny baby has cheated!" said Chortle on the loudspeaker.

"I haven't cheated!" I shouted. "We fought and I won round two!"

"The tiny baby has fought dirrrty and won rrround two," said Chortle. "Now we go back to Coney Island forrr rrround thrrree, which the mighty Gorrrgle will win!"

CHAPTER 12

By the time I got back to Coney Island, the people in the stands were cheering their heads off. I guess the helicopters had radioed ahead that I'd won round two. I saluted them. They cheered even harder. It was a good feeling.

Tortoise Man shook my hand. My mom and dad came up to me. I hoped they wouldn't hug me and blow my cover. They didn't.

"Great job, Max," whispered my dad.

"We're so proud of you, Max," whispered my mom.

"Way to go, little brother," said Tiffany. She gave me a high five.

"Thanks, guys," I said, "but it's not over yet. We still have round three."

The helicopters landed.

"The baby Drrrylanderrr fought dirrrty and cheated," said Chortle. "But the Waterrr People have no doubt we shall win rrround thrrree. So we shall allow the cheating baby Drrrylanderrr to prrretend he won rrround two."

"Let us continue the exams," said Puke-breath. "At what temperature does water boil?"

"I don't really have time for this now, Mr. Pukebreath," I said.

"You do, unless you wish to repeat the sixth grade," said Pukebreath.

He flashed me a nasty smile. He had me. I sighed.

"Water boils at . . . uh . . . let me see . . . 212 degrees Fahrenheit," I said. "OK?"

"Correct," said Pukebreath.

"All right, Chortle!" I yelled. "Since I won round two, I get to announce the challenge for round three!"

"That will not be necessarrry," Chortle answered.

"What do you mean?" I said.

"Next question," said Pukebreath. "At what temperature does water freeze?"

"Not now, Mr. Pukebreath," I said.

"So you'll be repeating the sixth grade, then?"

I sighed.

"Water freezes at thirty-two degrees Fahrenheit," I said to Pukebreath. "Chortle, what do you mean that won't be necessary?" I yelled.

"It will not be necessarrry because Gorrrgle has alrrready chosen the challenge forrr rrround thrrree."

"What do you mean he's chosen? He *can't* choose. It's *my* turn to choose."

"Too bad," said Chortle. "Gorrrgle has chosen."

"But that's cheating!"

"Oh, is the baby Drrrylanderrr the only one allowed to cheat?"

"What has Gorgle chosen?"

"Gorrrgle is even now swimming up to

the Arrrctic Cirrrcle. He will push the Polarrr Ice Cap down to the Equatorrr. The baby Drrrylanderrr will trrry to stop him. If the baby succeeds, the Drrrylanderrrs win the warrr. If Gorrrgle succeeds, the ice cap will melt and flood the earrrth."

Oh, no, this was terrible! The Water People were trying to destroy us, even before the war was over!

"OK, everybody," I said. "I'm off to the Arctic Circle. Wish me luck."

Everybody cheered and wished me luck.

I leaped into the air.

"One last question before you go," said Pukebreath. "I'm thinking of two numbers. Their sum is 8. Their product is 16. What is their difference?"

A math problem! Oh, no! I suddenly grew weak and dizzy. I crashed to the ground.

People in the stands groaned. Tortoise Man, my mom and dad, Tiffany, and other people rushed forward to help me.

"Pukebreath," I gasped. "Didn't they tell you . . . not to ask me . . . any math questions? You fool!"

Pukebreath laughed a nasty laugh.

"It is *you* who are the fool, Maximum Boy, not I," he said.

"W-what do you . . . mean?" I asked.

He laughed a crazy laugh. Then he grabbed his face with both hands and pulled. His face was a rubber mask. It came off. Pukebreath's real face was horrible. Pukebreath was . . . one of the Water People!

CHAPTER 13

Oh, no! So that's why he'd been bugging me so much with test questions. He really *was* trying to distract me. Why hadn't I realized it before?

The fake Pukebreath ripped off his clothes. Out flopped his enormous tail. That was what had made his butt look so big. Why hadn't I figured it out? Then, he threw away the voice box that had made his voice sound human.

The fake Pukebreath started to escape.

"Maximum Girl . . . grab him!" I said. I was so weak I could hardly speak.

Tiffany grabbed the fake Pukebreath by the ear and twisted.

"Ow!" he said. "You fight like a girrrl!"

"I *am* a girl," she said. "And you're, like, this really gross reptile."

"Way to go . . . Maximum Girl," I said.

"What have you done with the real Mr. Pukebreath, you creep?" asked Tiffany.

"Kidnapped him, of courrrse," said the creature. "You will neverrr find him in a thousand yearrrs! Not in a *million* yearrrs!"

Tiffany twisted his ear really hard.

"Ow!" said the fake Pukebreath. "Cut that out!"

"Tell me where you hid the real Mr. Pukebreath," she said. "Or else I'm going to, like, eat your ear with french fries and ketchup."

"All rrright, all rrright," he said. "I kidnapped him. Then I hid him in the Coney Island Aquarrrium. I made a rrrubberrr mold of his face and stole his clothing. It was a perrrfect plan. And what's morrre, it worrrked!"

"Not . . . yet . . . you creep," I said. "Maximum Girl . . . go to the Aquarium . . . and free Mr. Pukebreath. Then . . . take this creep . . . to jail."

"And what about you?" she asked.

"I'm . . . going to the Arctic Circle," I said.

"No way! You can't even walk!"

"I'm . . . not walking," I said. "I'm . . . flying."

It took a few minutes before the effects of the math problem wore off and I felt strong enough to jump back into the air. I flew up the coast to Canada. Then due north to the Arctic Circle. The helicopters followed me, but I flew above them.

The landscape below me was now nothing but white. One humongous sheet of ice known as the Polar Ice Cap. I was at the South Pole once. I was delivering ransom money to an evil scientist named Dr. Zirkon. I've never been to the North Pole, though. They looked exactly the same. I guess if you've seen one pole, you've pretty much seen them all.

I kept looking for Gorgle and not finding him. Which wasn't too surprising when you think about it. I mean I was flying over hundreds of miles of ice, and Gorgle was only ten feet tall. The air was very cold and very clear. I flew higher and higher. Now I could see for hundreds of miles in every direction.

I could see a whole lot of the Polar Ice Cap. I could see that there was a big crack in it that ran for miles. I could see that the crack was getting wider. And wider. Wait a minute. Why was there a crack in it, and why was it getting wider?

And then it hit me: The crack was getting wider because something was *making* it get wider. And that something was probably Gorgle.

The top part of the ice cap wasn't moving, but the bottom part was heading south fast. And then I realized what Gorgle had in mind. By breaking off the bottom part of the ice cap, he could make a right turn at Greenland. Then he could push it into the Atlantic, where he'd have a clear shot all the way down to the Equator.

As it got hotter, the ice would melt and cause floods that would wipe out everybody in its path. Everything on the East and West Coasts would disappear. I had to find Gorgle and stop him before that happened!

I heard the sound of helicopters. I dropped down about 1,000 feet and began flying along the crack. I still couldn't see Gorgle. Maybe he was pushing the ice cap from under the water.

Then, suddenly, I spotted Gorgle. He was a tiny black speck below me at the edge of the ice cap. I zoomed down and buzzed him like a fighter plane.

"Stop, Gorgle!" I shouted. "Stop in the

name of the United States Government! Stop in the name of the United Nations! Stop in the name of all the peoples of Earth!"

He didn't stop. I zoomed in low again and punched him in the face as I passed. Something whapped me on the back of the head and hurled me into the water. His tail!

Gorgle was on me in a flash. The water was freezing cold. He grabbed my throat with a huge clawed hand and began to squeeze. I couldn't breathe. I grabbed his wrist and used my superpowers to squeeze. With superpowers, my grip is stronger than an alligator's jaws. Gorgle screamed and let go of my throat. I let go of his wrist.

Out of the corner of my eye I saw something. Long wavy strands of something. Seaweed? No, but it looked familiar. Tentacles?

Yes! And then I knew what it was. Long tentacles of the box jellyfish, otherwise known as the sea wasp. We studied that in school, too, right after sharks.

Like sharks, jellyfish have been around longer than dinosaurs. Jellyfish have even been around longer than sharks. The sea wasp is one of the most poisonous creatures on Earth. One touch of its sixty-foot-long tentacles can kill a 200-pound man in less than ten minutes. One of those tentacles was inches away from my body!

The tentacle snaked toward me. I ducked and it brushed against Gorgle. He panicked. He began thrashing around in the water. I grabbed the edge of the ice cap and pulled myself out of the water. Gorgle followed. It looked like he was in pain.

"It is all overrr," he gasped. "I have been

stung by a sea wasp. The mighty Gorrrgle is dying. I congrrratulate you. Please grrrant me one final rrrequest."

"What?" I said.

"Have Chorrrtle tell my family I loved them."

"You have a family?" I said. Somehow I couldn't picture Gorgle with a family.

"A lovely wife. A pet turrrtle. Thrrrree adorrrable childrrren," said Gorgle. "I was a good fatherrr, I think."

He reached painfully under a flap in his armor and brought out a picture.

"Look," he said.

The picture was so wet I couldn't see a thing. Which was probably just as well.

"Look at those little ones," he said. "Don't they look just like theirrr papa?"

"Exactly," I said.

This was really confusing. I did want to beat Gorgle. I wanted that with all my might. But I don't think I wanted him to die. And that was even *before* I knew he had a wife and kids and a pet turtle.

"Listen, Gorgle," I said. "Maybe you don't have to die."

"Nonsense," said Gorgle. "The sting of a sea wasp's tentacle will kill a 200-pound man in ten minutes."

"You must have read the same book *I* did. But you're *not* a 200-pound man. You're a — what? — 500-pound Water Person. So maybe there's a way to save you."

"How?"

"Well, ammonia takes the poison out of most stings. Bees, hornets, jellyfish, and wasps — the flying kind. I'll bet it would help you, too."

"Wherrre would you get ammonia on the Polarrr Ice Cap?"

I pointed.

"Up there. In the helicopters. They probably clean their windshields with Windex. Windex has ammonia in it."

I flew up to the UN helicopter.

"You guys got any Windex?" I shouted over the sound of the engines. "Gorgle got stung by a sea wasp!"

The pilot of the helicopter shook his head in confusion, then handed me a spray bottle. I thanked him and flew down to the ice cap.

"Where did he sting you, Gorgle?"

Gorgle pointed to his butt. I sprayed where he was pointing.

"We arrre enemies," said Gorgle. "Why do you want to save me?"

"I don't know," I said. "Maybe it has something to do with your pet turtle."

I flew Gorgle up to the UN helicopter and loaded him on board. Then I flew down and pushed the Polar Ice Cap back where it belonged.

Everybody on Coney Island was pretty glad the way things turned out. My mom, dad, and Tiffany said they were really proud of me. I was in all the newspapers and all the radio and TV news programs for around a week.

Gorgle not only lived, he forced Chortle to make a formal apology to everybody on Earth. The Water People promised never to invade the Dry World again. We waved good-bye to them as they walked back into the ocean.

The real Irwin Pukebreath thanked Tiffany all over the place for saving him.

But his first words to *me* were: "Name the ten longest rivers of the world, in descending order of length."

ABOUT THE AUTHOR

When he was a kid, author Dan Greenburg used to be a lot like Maximum Boy — he lived with his parents and sister in Chicago, he was skinny, he wore glasses and braces, he was a lousy athlete, he was allergic to milk products, and he became dizzy when exposed to math problems. Unlike Maximum Boy, Dan was never able to lift locomotives or fly.

As an adult, Dan has written more than forty books for both kids and grown-ups, which have been reprinted in twenty-three countries. His kids' books include the series The Zack Files, which is also a TV series. His grown-up books include *How to Be a Jewish Mother* and *How to Make Yourself Miserable*. Dan has written for the movies and TV, the Broadway stage, and most national magazines. He has appeared on network TV as an author and comedian. He is still trying to lift locomotives and fly.